Disasters

Space Disasters and Earthquakes

逃出天災地劫

ANN WEIL

Development: Kent Publishing Services, Inc.
Design and Production: Signature Design Group, Inc.

Photo Credits: page 19, Stocktrek/Corbis; pages 29, 40, 41, Bettmann/Corbis; page
49, Roger Ressmyer/Corbis; page 58, KRT/NewsCom; page 66, Getty Images; page
67, Matt Stroshane/Getty Images; page 99, Richard Berenholtz/Corbis; page 107,
Owen Franken/Corbis; page 131, Bettemann/Corbis

書　　名：逃出天災地劫
　　　　　Space Disasters and Earthquakes
作　　者：Ann Weil
責　　編：黃家麗
封面設計：張　毅
出　　版：商務印書館 (香港) 有限公司
　　　　　香港筲箕灣耀興道 3 號東滙廣場 8 樓
　　　　　http://www.commercialpress.com.hk
發　　行：香港聯合書刊物流有限公司
　　　　　香港新界大埔汀麗路 36 號中華商務印刷大廈 3 字樓
印　　刷：中華商務彩色印刷有限公司
　　　　　香港新界大埔汀麗路 36 號中華商務印刷大廈 14 字樓
版　　次：2012 年 7 月第 1 版第 1 次印刷
　　　　　©2012 商務印書館 (香港) 有限公司
　　　　　ISBN 978 962 07 1968 4
　　　　　Printed in Hong Kong

版權所有　不得翻印

CONTENTS 目錄

Publisher's Note 出版說明......................................7

Usage Note 使用說明..8

Part 1
Space Disasters 太空事故

1 Introduction
遠征外太空...10

2 Apollo 1, 1967
電路走火燃燒阿波羅 1 號..................................20

3 Apollo 13, 1970
阿波羅 13 號爆炸，太空人奇蹟逃生....................30

4 Soyuz 11, 1971
聯合 11 號漏氣，太空人慘死..............................42

5 Challenger, 1986
現場直播挑戰者號爆炸.....................................50

6 Columbia, 2003
哥倫比亞號空中解體..60

7 Educator Astronaut
太空人老師..68

Exercises 練習

1 Vocabulary 詞彙

1.1 Multiple Meaning Words 多義詞 69

2 Initial Understanding 初步理解

2.1 Acronyms 縮寫詞 70

2.2 Everyday Acronyms 常用縮寫詞 71

3 Interpretation 解釋

3.1 Punctuation Makes A Difference
標點符號的重要 71

Part 2
Earthquakes 地震

1 Introduction
地動山搖 74

2 San Francisco 1906, 1989
火燒舊金山 86

3 Mexico City, 1985
墨西哥城瓦礫堆中的奇蹟 100

4 Japan, 1923, 1995
日本強震大火奪家園 108

5 Lisbon, 1755
巨浪席捲里斯本 116

6 China
中國唐山大地震 122

7 Preparing for Earthquakes
防患未然 132

Exercises 練習

I Vocabulary 詞彙

   I.I Word Sort 詞彙分類 133

   I.2 Fill in the Blanks 填充 133

2 Initial Understanding 初步理解

   2.I True or False? 是非題 134

3 Interpretation 解釋

   3.I Before, During, After 事發前後與經過 135

Answer Key
答案 137

English-Chinese Vocabulary List
中英對照生詞表 139

More to Read
延伸閱讀 144

Publisher's Note
出版說明

今年應該不是世界末日，但災難事故幾乎每天都在發生。怎樣用英語講述重大事故，Disasters 閱讀系列提供一個參考。

Disasters 閱讀系列是 Quality English Learning〈優質英語階梯閱讀〉的全新系列，與已推出兩套 16 本的〈*National Geographic* 百科英語階梯閱讀〉異曲同工，同為閱讀真實題材，學好生活英語。

系列分 Level 1 和 Level 2，共五本書，每本書含兩個災難主題，一共十個，包括：火山爆發、森林大火、太空事故、地震、空難、特大風暴、海難、登山遇險、恐怖襲擊、環境危機。用英語講解災難形成的前因後果，簡明扼要，以英漢對照形式，按時序介紹具代表性的災難，比如穿梭機哥倫比亞號如何解體、唐山大地震造成的巨大破壞等。

按主題解釋關鍵詞語，列出相關事實，以地圖標示災難發生的地點。閱讀之餘，可透過多樣化練習題自我測試。附中英對照生詞表，含專有名詞及常用詞語供快速查閱。

"閱讀真實題材，學好生活英語"是為特點。我們衷心希望本系列能幫助讀者提高英語表達能力。

商務印書館（香港）有限公司

編輯出版部

Usage Note
使用說明

Step 1

閱讀英漢對照的時間軸、重點詞彙、災難發生地點的地圖，概括理解主題。

Step 2

閱讀英語正文，了解災難事故的前因後果，有需要可看生詞、短語中譯，也可查閱中英對照生詞表及常用詞語。

Step 3

做練習題，自我測試英語能力。

Part 1

Space
Disasters
太空事故

1 Introduction
遠征外太空

April 12, 1961
Yuri Gagarin, Russian cosmonaut, is the first person to enter outer space.

1961 年 4 月 12 日
前蘇聯太空人尤里·加加林是第一個進入外太空的人。

July 20, 1969
Neil Armstrong is the first person to walk on the moon.

1969 年 7 月 20 日
尼爾·阿姆斯特朗成為首名在月球漫步的人。

Where is Russia? 俄羅斯在哪裏？ ▶▶▶

RUSSIA 俄羅斯

The International Space Station is the largest scientific project in world history. Astronauts from different nations work together in teams of three for months at a time.

國際太空站是有史以來最龐大的科學項目。來自不同國家的太空人，每次利用幾個月時間，三人一組的在國際太空站裏進行研究工作。

KEY TERMS 重點詞彙

astronaut - a person who is trained to go into outer space

太空人是受訓進入外太空的人

space station - a spacecraft that stays in space for a long time

太空站是長期停留在外太空的太空船

gravity - the force that pulls objects towards the centre of Earth

地球引力是把物體拉向地球中心的力量

cosmonaut - a Russian astronaut

前蘇聯太空人

Chapter One:
Introduction

On July 20, 1969, astronaut[1] Neil Armstrong[2] stepped onto the moon. Millions of people watched this amazing event on television.

No one had ever stood on the moon before. It changed how people thought about our planet and the universe.

Now, space travel doesn't seem so extraordinary[3]. A rocket[4] blasting off[5] isn't always big news anymore. Hundreds of astronauts and scientists have travelled in space.

---

1   astronaut, *n*：太空人
2   Neil Armstrong：尼爾・阿姆斯特朗
3   extraordinary, *adj*：特別的
4   rocket, *n*：火箭
5   blast off：發射

Some people have even become space tourists. They pay a lot of money to spend a week in space. Now, people even live in space for months at a time.

Science Fiction/Science Fact

It's hard to believe that less than 50 years ago, space travel was just a fantasy[1]. Science fiction books and movies put people in outer space. But it wasn't until 1961 that someone travelled into space.

Snapshot

Footprint on the surface of the moon

月球表面的腳印

The first person to go into space was a Russian man named Yuri Gagarin[2]. He

---

1   fantasy, *n*：幻想

2   Yuri Gagarin：尤里・加加林

orbited[1] Earth once in a Russian rocket. Then he landed safely.

Not every space mission[2] has gone so well. Some space accidents damage very expensive equipment[3]. Even a minor accident can cost millions of dollars. This can be a disaster for a country's space program.

Space travel is risky. Some astronauts have died in space accidents. The total number of space-related deaths is low. But these tragedies[4] seem much bigger. Fortunately, there are very few space disasters.

The First Space Stations

The first space stations[5] were small laboratories[6] that orbited Earth. Astro-nauts travelled to the space station in

---

1 orbit, *v*：沿軌道運行
2 mission, *n*：任務
3 equipment, *n*：設備
4 tragedy, *n*：悲劇
5 space station：太空站
6 laboratory, *n*：實驗室

rockets. They lived and worked in space for months at a time.

There is no gravity[1] in space. People and things are weightless[2]. Scientists studied the effects of living in space on people and other living things. They learned a lot from experiments[3] on these early space stations.

The Russians built the first space station. *Salyut 1*[4] was launched[5] on April 19, 1971. The American space station, *Skylab*[6], was launched two years later, in May 1973.

The Russians launched their eighth space station, *Mir*[7], in February, 1986. *Mir* means "peace" in Russian. Mir cosmonauts[8] became the first people to spend more than a year in space.

There were many problems with the early space stations. Some of these turned

---

1   gravity, *n*：地球引力

2   weightless, *adj*：無重量的

3   experiment, *n*：實驗

4   *Salyut 1*：敬禮 1 號

5   launch, *v*：發射

6   *Skylab*：天空實驗室

7   *Mir*：和平號

8   cosmonaut, *n*：前蘇聯太空人

into disasters. But the lessons learned from these catastrophes[1] helped make the newest space station — the *International Space Station* — better and safer.

The International Space Station

Americans and Russians work with astronauts and scientists from other countries on the *International Space tation*. They do many different scientific experiments. The results of these experiments can help us learn more about life in space and life on Earth.

The *International Space Station* (ISS) orbits the Earth. Astronauts live and work on the ISS for about three to six months. Then a new crew[2] comes to the ISS to continue the work.

The ISS is the only space station orbiting Earth. The earlier space stations are no longer in orbit.

---

1   catastrophe, *n*：大災難
2   crew, *n*：組員

Skylab in Trouble!

Skylab was launched on May 14, 1973. It was more than three times larger than *Salyut 1* and weighed about 100 tons. But only one minute after taking off [1], *Skylab* was in serious trouble. A big meteor shield[2] fell off. It tore away[3] a large screen of solar panels[4]. NASA[5] launched a team of three astronauts to fix the space station. The astronauts fixed the problem while *Skylab* orbited Earth.

---

1 take off：起飛
2 meteor shield：隕石防護盾
3 tear away：扯落
4 solar panel, *n*：太陽能板
5 NASA：美國太空總署

Snapshot

In the International Space Station, there are two crew cabins. Each cabin is large enough for one astronaut to sleep in.

國際太空站裏有兩個駕駛艙。每個駕駛艙有足夠一個太空人居住的空間。

19

2 Apollo 1, 1967
電路走火燃燒阿波羅 1 號

Timeline 時間軸

December 3, 1967

The first successful heart transplant is performed.

1967 年 12 月 3 日
首宗心臟移植手術成功。

January 27, 1967

A fire breaks out in the command module during practice for the Apollo 1 mission into space.

1967 年 1 月 27 日
阿波羅 1 號進行太空任務演習時，指揮艙失火。

Where is the NASA launch pad?
美國太空總署發射台在哪裏？

NASA LAUNCH PAD 美國太空總署發射台 ➜

DID YOU KNOW? 你知道嗎？

In 1965, Ed White became the first American to perform the "spacewalk." He floated outside the spacecraft for 23 minutes.

愛德華・懷特在1965年成為第一位在太空漫步的美國人。他在太空艙外漂浮了23分鐘。

KEY TERMS 重點詞彙

Soviet Union - a country that existed from 1922 to 1991 in eastern Europe. Russia was a part of the Soviet Union.

蘇聯是一個存在於1922年至1991年的東歐國家。俄羅斯是蘇聯的一部分。

National Aeronautics and Space Administration (NASA) - an organization whose mission is to plan space activities

美國太空總署是一個專門策劃太空項目及任務的組織

command module - the place where the astronauts control the spaceship

指揮艙是太空人控制太空船的地方

hatch - a door in the command module

艙口是指揮艙的門

Chapter Two:
Apollo 1, 1967

The United States and the Soviet Union[1] had space programs in the 1960s. Now both countries work together on the *International Space Station*. But, in the 1960s, they did not work together. They competed against[2] each other. Each country wanted to be the first to rule space.

At first, the Russians were ahead in the race to space. The first person in space was Russian cosmonaut Yuri Gagarin. The United States had to catch up to[3] the Soviet Union before they could take the lead in the space race.

The Birth of NASA

American President[4] John F. Kennedy wanted the first person on the moon to be

---

1 Soviet Union：蘇聯
2 compete against：競爭
3 catch up to：趕上
4 president, *n*：總統

an American. The National Aeronautics and Space Administration (NASA)[1] was created in July 1958.

Its official mission was to plan and conduct[2] space activities. Its real goal was to land American astronauts on the moon and return them safely to Earth.

The first two NASA projects[3] were named Mercury and Gemini. The Mercury and Gemini projects put Americans into outer space. The third project, named Apollo[4], would land them on the moon.

The first Apollo spaceship[5] was scheduled to take off on February 21, 1967. Thousands of people at NASA were working very hard to make that happen. It was supposed to be a great moment. Instead, the Apollo program began with tragedy.

---

1   National Aeronautics and Space Administration (NASA)：
    美國太空總署
2   conduct, v：執行
3   project, n：工程
4   Apollo：阿波羅
5   spaceship, n：太空船

A Fateful Test

On January 27, 1967, the *Apollo 1*[1] crew was practising for their trip into space. The crew consisted of[2] Gus Grissom, Ed White, and Roger Chaffee. Grissom and White had both been into space before. *Apollo 1* was Chaffee's first mission in space.

The three astronauts were inside the command module[3] of the spaceship. The command module is like the cockpit[4] of a plane. It's where the astronauts sit to control the spaceship.

They were testing the plan for lift off[5]. The astronauts were strapped[6] into their seats. The command module was locked and sealed[7].

The astronauts could talk to the NASA

---

1 *Apollo 1*：阿波羅 1 號
2 consist of：包括
3 command module：指揮艙
4 cockpit, *n*：駕駛艙
5 lift off：升空
6 strap, *v*：被綁住
7 seal, *v*：密封

team using a communications system[1]. But the system was not working properly. NASA technicians[2] outside the command module were trying to fix that. Everything else seemed fine.

No Escape

Then, suddenly, a fire broke out[3] inside the command module. The astronauts reported the emergency[4]. One of them tried to open the hatch[5] to the outside. That was the only way to escape. But the hatch was stuck. The astronauts were trapped[6] inside!

The flames spread quickly. The fire burned the walls of the command module. Poisonous[7] smoke filled the inside of the command module. The fire was so hot,

---

1　communications system：通訊系統
2　technician, n：技術人員
3　break out：起火
4　emergency, n：緊急事故
5　hatch, n：艙門
6　trap, v：被困
7　poisonous, adj：有毒的

the command module cracked. That made a very loud noise. It sounded like an explosion[1].

Technicians grabbed fire extinguishers[2]. They tried to put out the fire[3]. But smoke from the fire made it difficult to breathe[4]. Some of them found gas masks[5].

Others tried to help without gas masks. It was very difficult. There was so much smoke, they could not see. They had to open the hatches using only their sense of touch[6].

There were three hatches on the command module. It took almost five minutes to open them all. By then, the three astronauts were dead.

No one knows exactly when or how they died. They probably died quickly from breathing poisonous smoke. Or they might have burned to death.

---

1   explosion, *n*：爆炸
2   fire extinguisher, *n*：滅火器
3   put out the fire：滅火
4   breathe, *v*：呼吸
5   gas mask：防毒面具
6   sense of touch：觸覺

The heat inside the command module was very intense[1]. It had melted their space suits[2]. The fire had also melted the nylon[3] from the seats. At first, no one could move the dead bodies. They were stuck to the seats.

The Investigation

The *Apollo 1* fire was a disaster for NASA. Plans for the *Apollo 1* launch were put on hold[4].

There was an investigation[5]. But the cause of the fire was never discovered. The most likely explanation was that a spark[6] from bad electrical wiring[7] started the fire.

The spark ignited[8] oxygen gas inside the command module. There was a very high level of oxygen inside the command module. Oxygen burns quickly.

---

1   intense, *adj*：強烈的

2   space suit, *n*：太空衣

3   nylon, *n*：尼龍

4   put on hold：暫停

5   investigation, *n*：調查

6   spark, *n*：火花

7   electrical wiring：電路

8   ignite, *v*: 使燃燒

The tragedy was also the result of poor planning and design. Many safety changes were made following the *Apollo 1* disaster. A new fast-release escape hatch[1] was put in the command module. The new hatch could be opened from inside in seven seconds.

The Apollo program was delayed by 21 months. But it did recover[2] after the tragic fire. *Apollo 11* astronauts Neil Armstrong and Buzz Aldrin were the first people to walk on the moon. Five other Apollo missions also put people on the surface of the moon.

The late President Kennedy's wish was realized[3]. And despite its tragic beginning, the Apollo program was a tremendous[4] success.

---

1 fast-release escape hatch：速開逃生門
2 recover, *v*：恢復
3 be realized：獲得實現
4 tremendous：巨大的

Snapshot

Apollo 1 astronauts (L-R), Virgil "Gus" Grissom, Edward White, and Roger Chaffee, suited up at the Saturn launch pad. A few days later, all three would be killed in an electrical fire in the command module during testing.

阿波羅1號的太空人（由左至右）維吉爾·格里森，愛德華·懷特，及羅傑·查菲穿戴整齊地站在土星發射台。幾日後，他們三人在控制艙試驗中，因電線走火而喪生。

3 Apollo 13, 1970
阿波羅 13 號爆炸，太空人奇蹟逃生

Timeline 時間軸

April 11, 1970

Apollo 13 lifts off on a mission to the moon.

1970 年 4 月 11 日
阿波羅 13 號升空展開登月任務。

April 13, 1970

There is an explosion on the *Apollo 13*.

1970 年 4 月 13 日
阿波羅13號發生爆炸。

Where is the Pacific Ocean? 太平洋在哪裏？

PACIFIC OCEAN 太平洋

DID YOU KNOW? 你知道嗎？

The astronauts on board *Apollo 13* ran out of water. They drank less than one cup of water each day.

阿波羅13號上的太空人食水短缺。每天只能飲用最多一杯的水。

KEY TERMS 重點詞彙

German measles - a disease that causes the neck to become swollen and the skin to develop red spots

德國痲疹是一種疾病，有全身出紅疹及淋巴腫脹的病徵。

lunar module - a separate structure designed to land the astronauts on the moon

登月艙是一個可獨立運作的交通工具，用來載送太空人登陸月球。

Chapter Three:
Apollo 13, 1970

The *Apollo* 11 astronauts were the first people to walk on the moon. Millions of people knew the names Neil Armstrong and Buzz Aldrin[1].

Apollo 12 astronauts also landed on the moon. *Apollo 13* was going to be the third time American astronauts walked on the moon.

But *Apollo 13* never landed on the moon. Two days after it took off from Earth, *Apollo 13* was in trouble. A tank of oxygen exploded[2].

The blast damaged the spacecraft[3]. It looked as though the astronauts would not be able to return to Earth. They might be stranded[4] in space!

---

1 Buzz Aldrin：巴茲・奧爾德林
2 explode, *v*：爆炸
3 spacecraft, *n*：太空船
4 strand, *v*：滯留於

Unlucky 13?

Some people believe the number 13 is unlucky[1]. The explosion on *Apollo 13* happened on the 13th of April. But the mission's bad luck began even before the spacecraft took off.

Three days before launch, there was a last-minute crew change. The *Apollo 13* crew was accidentally exposed to[2] German measles[3].

Two of the crew had already had the disease. They could not get it again. But the command module pilot had never had German measles.

NASA doctors were afraid he would get sick during the mission. They would not let him go on the mission. The back-up pilot[4], Jack Swigert, replaced him.

---

1   unlucky, *adj*：不吉祥的
2   expose to：使感染
3   German measles：德國痲疹
4   back-up pilot：後備駕駛員

Swigert was an experienced[1] pilot. But he had not been training with the other two crew members. Space missions depend on[2] excellent teamwork. The three astronauts had to learn how to work together. And they had only two days to get used to[3] each other.

Three…two…one…lift off!

Apollo 13 lifted off on April 11, 1970. At first everything went well. All systems were working properly.

On their third day in space, the astronauts made a TV broadcast[4]. They showed how they lived and worked in space. People back on Earth could see what it was like to be weightless.

But less than ten minutes after they finished this, something went very wrong.

---

1   experienced, *adj*：有經驗的
2   depend on：依賴
3   get used to：熟悉
4   TV broadcast：電視廣播

There was a sharp bang[1]. The spaceship shook. Warning lights[2] in the command module showed that two of the three fuel supplies[3] were gone. The fuel provided electricity[4] for everything on the spacecraft.

The astronauts quickly realized they would not be able to land on the moon. There wasn't enough power left. They were terribly disappointed[5].

Then they saw that their oxygen supplies[6] were dangerously low. One of the astronauts looked out the window. He saw the oxygen gas spraying[7] out of the spacecraft.

This was much more serious than not landing on the moon. They needed this oxygen to breathe. Without it, they would

---

1　bang, *n*：砰的一聲
2　warning light, *n*：警示燈
3　fuel supply：燃料電池
4　electricity, *n*：電力
5　disappointed, *adj*：失望
6　supply, *n*：供給
7　spray, *v*：噴出

die. And without power, the spacecraft would not be able to get them home.

The three astronauts realized that making it back to Earth alive would be a miracle[1].

No Air, No Water, No Power

The astronauts lost most of their oxygen within three hours. They also lost their water.

There was almost no power left. The command module was supposed to be the astronaut's control centre in space. Now it was useless.

But the lunar module[2] was still attached. This was the astronauts' only hope. They moved into the lunar module. It became their lifeboat[3] in space.

---

1   miracle, *n*：奇蹟
2   lunar module：登月艙
3   lifeboat, *n*：救生艇

Lunar Module Lifeboat

The lunar module had its own supply of oxygen. It also had a separate power supply.

The explosion had not affected the lunar module. It still had oxygen and power. But would it be enough to keep the astronauts alive till they could return safely to Earth?

The lunar module was designed[1] to land two astronauts on the moon. After two days on the moon, the two astronauts would return to the command module. The third astronaut would remain[2] in the command module.

Now all three astronauts needed to live in the lunar module. It would take them four days to get back to Earth.

The lunar module was not designed to support three astronauts for four days. Still, it was the only way the astronauts could survive their trip back to Earth.

---

1 design, v：設計
2 remain, v：留待

They had to make it work.

Struggle for Survival

The astronauts had enough oxygen to breathe. They circled the moon. Then they used the power left in the lunar module to push themselves back toward Earth.

They were on their way home. But there was very little water. Each astronaut drank less than a cup of water a day. That was less than a fifth of what they were supposed to drink.

There was no power to heat the space-craft. The astronauts were freezing[1] cold.

There was no hot water to put in their food either. Space food is usually dehy-drated[2]. Normally the astronauts would add hot water to the food, then eat it. But without hot water, the food was useless. The astronauts ate very little.

---

1   freezing, *adj*：極冷的

2   dehydrated, *adj*：脫水的

It was a long, cold, hungry four days. But the astronauts returned safely to Earth on April 17. They splashed down[1] into the Pacific Ocean. They were tired, hungry, and thirsty. One of the astronauts had lost 14 pounds. But they were alive, and very happy to be home.

A Successful Failure?

The *Apollo 13* mission did not land on the moon. It was a $375 million failure[2]. But everyone was very relieved the three astronauts were safe. Getting them home alive under the circumstances[3] was a tremendous achievement[4].

1　splash down：濺落
2　failure, *n*：失敗
3　circumstance, *n*：情勢
4　achievement, *n*：成就

Snapshot

Navy swimmers fasten a floatation collar around the Apollo 13 capsule as it floats after splashdown in the Pacific Ocean.

美國海軍在阿波羅13號太空艙濺落太平洋海面後，
立即為太空艙繫上浮圈。

Snapshot

Left to right: Fred Haise, lunar module pilot; James Lovell, commander; and Jack Swigert, command module pilot, wave to a crowd after their successful splashdown.

由左至右：登月艙駕駛員弗萊德・海斯；指揮官吉姆・洛威爾；指揮艙駕駛員傑克・斯威格特，在成功濺落後和大眾揮手。

4 Soyuz 11, 1971
聯合 11 號漏氣，太空人慘死

Timeline 時間軸

April 19, 1971
Salyut 1, the world's first space station, is launched.

1971 年 4 月 19 日
世上第一個太空站敬禮 1 號發射。

April 23, 1971
The first space station crew leaves for Salyut 1.

1971 年 4 月 23 日
第一批太空站機員出發至敬禮1號。

Where is Soviet Union? 蘇聯在哪裏？ ▶▶▶

SOVIET UNION 蘇聯

DID YOU KNOW? 你知道嗎？

Vladimir M. Komarov was the first person to die in a space mission, in 1967. While returning to Earth, the main parachute did not open. The rocket crashed into the ground.

弗拉迪米爾·科馬洛夫是首位執行太空任務時遇難的人。在1967年返回地球途中，主要降落傘因故障未能打開，導致太空艙墜毀。

KEY TERMS 重點詞彙

valve - a device that controls the flow of a gas

氣閥是控制空氣流量的儀器

suffocate - to stop a person from breathing

窒息是使一個人停止呼吸

space suit - a special suit that allows astronauts to survive in space

太空衣是讓太空人可在外太空生存的特別衣服

Chapter Four:
Soyuz 11, 1971

The Russians knew they could not win the moon race. Instead, they focused on building the first space station. They launched *Salyut 1* in April 1971.

Salyut 1 was the world's first space station. *Salyut* means "salute" in Russian. The name was chosen in memory of [1] cosmonaut Yuri Gagarin. Gagarin was the first person in space. He was a Russian hero[2]. In 1968, Gagarin was killed in a plane crash[3].

Soyuz

The *Salyut 1* space station was launched without anyone inside. Cosmonauts travelled to the space station on a small

---

1   in memory of：為了紀念

2   hero, *n*：英雄

3   plane crash, *n*：墜機

rocket ship called *Soyuz*[1]. *Soyuz* means "union" in Russian. These rockets could make one trip up into space and back. A new Soyuz rocket was used for each trip.

The first crew arrived at *Salyut 1* four days after the space station was launched. But they did not get inside. They could not open the hatch. They came back to Earth without entering the space station.

The second crew did get into the space station. This was the first time a space station was occupied[2]. The three cosmonauts stayed on *Salyut 1* for 23 days. That was the longest anyone had ever been in space. The Russians were very proud of this achievement.

Space Science

Space stations are like small laboratories. The cosmonauts did experiments. They wanted to see how people reacted[3] to

---

1 *Soyuz*：聯合號
2 occupy, *v*：使用
3 react, *v*：反應

being in space for long periods of time.

They studied themselves to find out how their bodies reacted to being weightless. They also studied Earth's weather. The information they gathered would help improve weather forecasts[1].

The cosmonauts completed their experiments. It was time for them to leave the space station. They boarded[2] their Soyuz rocket.

The rocket separated from the space station. It orbited Earth three times. The cosmonauts were ready to come back to Earth.

It seemed like their mission was a complete success. But disaster was about to strike. The three men would not make it back to Earth alive.

---

1   forecast, *n*：預報
2   board, *v*：登機

Dead on Arrival

Mission Control[1] tried to contact the cosmonauts as they returned to Earth. But there was no answer. Still, everything seemed all right.

Soyuz rockets were programmed[2] to return to Earth. The crew did not have to pilot[3] the rocket back to Earth.

The Soyuz 11 landed on schedule[4]. The ground crew opened the hatch. They were ready to welcome the three heroes home.

But instead they had a horrible shock. The three men were dead. They had died in space.

At first, these deaths were a mystery[5]. No one knew what had happened. The cosmonauts were found still strapped in their seats. There were no signs that they had tried to get out.

1　Mission Control：任務控制中心
2　program, v：輸入電腦程式
3　pilot, v：駕駛
4　on schedule：按預定時間
5　mystery, n：秘密

One idea was that they had all suffered heart attacks[1]. But that was not what happened. The tragedy was caused by a fault[2] in the rocket.

A valve[3] opened by accident. The air inside the rocket rushed out. The three men suffocated[4] to death.

If they had been wearing space suits, they would have survived. But the *Soyuz 11* was very small. The three cosmonauts were squeezed[5] inside.

There was not enough room for them to wear space suits. They relied on air inside the rocket to breathe. But when the valve opened, all the air escaped. They could not breathe, so they died.

---

1   heart attack, *n*：心臟病發
2   fault, *n*：故障
3   valve, *n*：氣閥
4   suffocate, *v*：窒息
5   squeeze, *v*：強擠

This disaster delayed the Soviet space program. The Soviet Union did not send a new crew to *Salyut 1*. Two years passed before they sent any more cosmonauts into space. And from then on, all cosmonauts wore spacesuits for launch and landing.

Snapshot

Launch of a Soyuz Mission, June 24, 1982

1982年6月24日聯合號發射。

5 Challenger, 1986
現場直播挑戰者號爆炸

Timeline 時間軸

April 12, 1981
The first space shuttle, *Columbia*, is launched.

1981 年 4 月 12 日
第一架太空穿梭機哥倫比亞號首次發射。

January 28, 1986
The *Challenger* space shuttle explodes less than two minutes after lift off.

1986 年 1 月 28 日
挑戰者號太空穿梭機升空不到兩分鐘後爆炸。

Where is New Hampshire? 新罕布什爾州在哪裏？

NEW HAMPSHIRE　新罕布什爾州

DID YOU KNOW? 你知道嗎？

It takes a space shuttle about ten minutes to get into its low orbit at 115 miles above Earth.

一架太空穿梭機需要大約十分鐘才能進入距離地面高度有115英里的近地軌道。

KEY TERMS 重點詞彙

space shuttle - a reusable spacecraft that lifts off like a rocket and lands like an airplane

太空穿梭機能像火箭升空，像飛機降落，是可以重複使用的航天器

Teacher in Space Program (TISP) - a NASA program designed to give teachers a chance to go into space

太空教師計劃是美國太空總署執行的計劃，讓教師可以體驗外太空。

ground - to stop

擱淺

seal - a cap placed over the lid of a container

密封環是於容器蓋子上再加蓋

Chapter Five:
Challenger, 1986

The American space shuttle[1] takes off like a rocket. It orbits the Earth like a spacecraft. And it lands like an airplane.

NASA started the space shuttle program in the 1970s. They wanted a spacecraft that could carry heavy loads[2] into space. They also wanted this new spacecraft to be reusable[3].

Previous spacecraft could be used only once. These early American and Russian rockets could make only one trip into space and back.

The same space shuttle can be used again and again. It can also carry very large, heavy objects. It brings satellites[4] and parts

---

1　space shuttle：太空穿梭機
2　load, *n*：貨物
3　reusable, *adj*：可重複使用的
4　satellite, *n*：人造衛星

of the *International Space Station* up into space to orbit[1] Earth.

The first space shuttle, *Columbia*[2], lifted off on April 12, 1981. Since then, there have been more than a hundred successful space shuttle missions. But the most famous space shuttle mission was a disaster.

Space Shuttle *Challenger*

Challenger was NASA's second space shuttle. It started flying in 1982. It successfully completed nine missions.

Challenger's tenth mission was the 25th space shuttle flight. *Challenger* was originally scheduled to lift off January 22, 1986. But there were many delays.

Bad weather and strong winds were partly to blame. There were also problems with the space shuttle itself. Part of the hatch had to be sawed off when it could

---

1   orbit, *v*：繞軌道運行
2   *Columbia*：哥倫比亞號

not be removed any other way. There were other problems, too. One of the fire monitors[1] was not working properly.

Finally, almost a week late, *Challenger* lifted off. But its flight would last less than two minutes and end in tragedy.

A Teacher in Space

Usually only NASA astronauts and scientists go up on the space shuttle. But the tenth *Challenger* mission was special. It was the first flight of a new NASA program called the Teacher in Space Program (TISP)[2].

The *Challenger* was scheduled to carry Sharon Christa McAuliffe, the first teacher to fly in space. Christa McAuliffe was a high school[3] teacher from New Hampshire[4]. She was going to teach lessons from space to students around the

---

1   monitor, *n*：監視器
2   Teacher in Space Program (TISP)：太空教師計劃
3   high school：高中
4   New Hampshire：新罕布什爾州

country.

More than 11,000 teachers applied to TISP. They all wanted to go up on the space shuttle. McAuliffe trained for many months before the flight.

She was very excited about the opportunity[1] to be part of the space program. Her students were very proud of their teacher.

The lift off was broadcast live[2]. TVs were turned on in schools all over the country so children could watch the *Challenger* lift off as it happened. They watched the *Challenger* lift off. And they saw it destroyed in a puff of smoke[3].

Challenger blew apart[4] 73 seconds after it took off. The space shuttle and its seven-person crew were lost.

Millions of people watched this disaster

---

1 opportunity, *n*：機會
2 broadcast live：現場直播
3 puff of smoke：一縷青煙
4 blow apart：爆炸解體

as it happened on television. It was a horrible shock. It left America, and the world, stunned[1] and sad.

A Terrible Loss

NASA had never lost an astronaut in flight[2]. Now it lost an entire seven-person crew.

The entire space shuttle program was grounded[3]. NASA had to figure out what went wrong. They needed to make sure the same thing wouldn't happen to the other space shuttles.

They looked closely at pictures of the *Challenger* blasting off. There was a puff of smoke coming from one of the rocket boosters[4] less than a second after take off.

---

1   stun, *adj*：震驚
2   in flight：飛行中
3   ground, *v*：擱淺
4   booster, *n*：助推器

Computer images confirmed there was a problem with one of the solid rocket booster seals[1]. Hot gas leaked out. This started a fire. The fire caused the fuel to explode within the rocket, which destroyed the space shuttle.

New Safety Plans

NASA made many changes after the *Challenger* disaster. They fixed the seals in the other space shuttles. New, stricter[2] safety plans were put into effect[3].

NASA built a new space shuttle in 1991. The *Endeavour*[4] replaced *Challenger*. Once again, NASA had a fleet[5] of four space shuttles.

---

1   seal, *n*：密封環
2   stricter, *adj*：更嚴謹的
3   put into effect：生效
4   *Endeavour*：奮進號
5   fleet, *n*：機羣

Snapshot

Space shuttle Challenger exploding in flight.

挑戰者號太空穿梭機在飛行中爆炸。

6 Columbia, 2003
哥倫比亞號空中解體

February 1, 2003
Columbia explodes as it returns to Earth.

2003 年 2 月 1 日
哥倫比亞號返回地球途中爆炸。

April 16, 2003
Columbia Space Shuttle Program Director, Ron Dittemore, decides to leave his job. He was director for 26 years.

2003 年 4 月 16 日
哥倫比亞號穿梭機計劃的主管迪特摩爾決定
辭職，離開擔任26年的主管工作。

Where is Texas? 得克薩斯州在哪裏？ ▶▶▶

TEXAS 得克薩斯州

DID YOU KNOW? 你知道嗎？

After the Columbia exploded, NASA planned a 555,000-acre search in Texas and Louisiana. The searchers looked for pieces of the shuttle on land, sea, and even in the air.

哥倫比亞號爆炸後，美國太空總署即展開搜索計劃，在得克薩斯州和路易斯安那州 555,000 英畝的陸地、海面，甚至天空裏尋找太空穿梭機的殘骸。

KEY TERMS 重點詞彙

bail out - to escape

擺脫困境，逃脫

parachute - a piece of material that opens like an umbrella to give a person a safe landing

降落傘是一個展開後如傘的裝置，讓人安全由空中降落

experiment - a scientific test

實驗是指科學試驗

Chapter Six:
Columbia, 2003

The second shuttle disaster happened in February 2003. Space shuttle *Columbia*[1] blew apart as it was returning to Earth.

The Crew

Seven astronauts were on board[2] Columbia when it exploded. Six were Americans. Rick Husband was the commander[3]. William McCool was the pilot. The other American astronauts were Kalpana Chawla, Michael Anderson, David Brown, and Laurel Clark. The seventh astronaut was from Israel[4]. His name was Ilan Ramon. Ramon was a colonel[5] in the Israeli Air Force[6]. This was the first time an Israeli astronaut had gone

---

1　Columbia：哥倫比亞號
2　on board：在機上
3　commander, *n*：指揮官
4　Israel：以色列
5　colonel, *n*：上校
6　Air Force, *n*：空軍

into space.

Only three of the *Columbia* astronauts had been in space before. It was the first trip for Brown, Clark, McCool, and Ramon.

Astronauts wear special suits when they return to Earth. These suits have a parachute[1]. But *Columbia* blew apart so quickly there was no time for the crew to bail out[2].

Small Holes, Big Trouble

This disaster happened just 16 minutes before *Columbia* was supposed to land. The outside of the space shuttle gets very, very hot as it comes down to Earth. Special tiles[3] protect the space shuttle and the astronauts from this heat. But this time, something went wrong. Super hot gas got inside the left wing of the shuttle. This caused the shuttle to blow apart.

---

1   parachute, *n*：降落傘
2   bail out：逃脱
3   tile, *n*：瓷磚

NASA wanted to know what caused these small holes. There were several possibilities[1]. During lift-off, a piece of foam[2] broke off and hit the wing. This may have damaged tiles that protect the shuttle when it comes back to Earth. Or maybe something else hit the shuttle and made a hole.

Columbia's 28th Mission

The *Columbia* astronauts were almost home when their mission turned to tragedy. They had been in space for 16 days. Some astronauts are also scientists. Their job is to complete experiments in space. Many of these focus on how the human body reacts to being in space. On this mission, astronauts were studying why people lose bone[3] and muscle[4] when they stay in space.

---

1 possibility, *n*：可能
2 foam, *n*：泡沫材料
3 bone, *n*：骨頭
4 muscle, *n*：肌肉

They also studied spiders[1]. Students in Australia had prepared that experiment. They were testing whether spiders can spin webs[2] in zero gravity.

Picking up the Pieces

Some people on the ground heard a loud boom[3] when the *Columbia* exploded. They saw pieces of the space shuttle fall to the ground. Luckily, no one was hurt by the falling pieces.

Pieces from the space shuttle were scattered[4] over a very large area. Thousands of police, soldiers, and volunteers[5] collected as many as they could find. NASA hopes that studying what's left of the shuttle will help them answer more questions about what happened.

1   spider, *n*：蜘蛛
2   spin web：織網
3   boom, *n*：隆隆聲
4   scatter, *v*：分散
5   volunteer, *n*：義工

Snapshot

The crew of the space shuttle Columbia *walk onto the launch pad. In the first row, pilot William McCool (left) and commander Rick Husband (right). In the second row are mission specialists Kalpana Chawla (left) and Laurel Clark (right). In the last row, payload specialist Ilan Ramon, payload commander Michael Anderson and mission specialist David Brown. Ilan Ramon was the first Israeli astronaut to travel into space.*

哥倫比亞號穿梭機的組員站在發射台。第一排左邊是駕駛威廉·麥庫爾，右邊是指揮官瑞克·赫斯本。最後一排有載荷專家伊蘭·拉蒙，載荷指揮官邁克爾·安德森，和任務專家大衛·布朗。伊蘭·拉蒙是以色列第一位上太空的太空人。

Snapshot

Columbia *was the first space shuttle. Its first trip into space was in 1981. Here the shuttle* Columbia *lifts off for its last mission on January 16, 2003. The* Columbia *was lost when it broke up upon re-entry to Earth on February 1, 2003. The disaster happened at the end of* Columbia's *28th trip.*

哥倫比亞號是第一架太空穿梭機。在1981年時第一次上太空。圖中是哥倫比亞號在2003年1月16日最後一次任務升空時拍攝的。哥倫比亞號在2003年2月1日,準備結束它第二十八次航程返回地球的途中,爆炸解體。

7 Educator Astronaut
太空人老師

After the *Challenger* exploded, Christa McAuliffe's back-up kept working with NASA. Her name is Barbara Morgan[1].She was a teacher from Idaho[2]. Morgan traveleed across the country. She talked with teachers and students about her time with NASA. Now Barbara Morgan is a full-time astronaut.

In 2003, NASA formed the Educator Astronaut Program[3]. Educator Astronauts talk with students while they are in space. The Internet and videos are two ways they do this. Students can tell NASA about a teacher they think would be a good Educator Astronaut.

You can support the Educator Astronauts by going online and joining the Earth Crew[4]. The Earth Crew completes missions here on Earth.

1　Barbara Morgan：芭芭拉・摩根
2　Idaho：愛達荷州
3　Educator Astronaut Program：太空人老師計劃
4　Earth Crew：地球組員

Exercises 練習

1 Vocabulary 詞彙

1.1 Multiple Meaning Words 多義詞

下列句子裏粗體字是多義詞，請圈出符合句子意思的詞彙解釋。請見示範。

1. The **hatch** was the only way to leave the spaceship.
   - (A.) an opening
   - B. to come out of an egg

2. The ISS orbits **Earth**.
   - A. soil, the land surface
   - B. the third planet from the sun

3. The **late** President Kennedy's wish for NASA to put a man on the moon happened.
   - A. not on time
   - B. dead

4. The first **crew** to *Salyut 1* couldn't get in.
   - A. to work as a member of a team
   - B. members of a team

5. As they were afraid the pilot would get sick, NASA used the **back-up**.
   - A. a substitute
   - B. an overflow caused by a blockage

6. Oxygen **gas** sprayed out of the spacecraft.
   - A. a natural fuel
   - B. matter not in solid or liquid form

7. There was no time for the Columbia crew to **bail out**.
   A. to remove water from
   B. to escape

2 Initial Understanding 初步理解

2.1 Acronyms 縮寫詞

英文的技術專有名詞常被縮略為縮寫詞，由詞的首字母組合而成。下列詞語若是縮寫詞的請打勾，並從 A-E 的選擇中找出適當的解釋。請見示範。

√	1. NASA	E
	2. ISS	_____
	3. LEM	_____
	4. Mir	_____
	5. TISP	_____

A. lunar excursion module or the vehicle for travelling on the moon

B. the International Space Station, a spacecraft for astronauts throughout the world

C. teachers in space program through NASA

D. a Russian space station, the name means peace

E. National Aeronautics and Space Administration, the U.S.'s *space* program

2.2 Everyday Acronyms 常見縮寫詞

日常生活中也有很多縮寫詞。從網上或字典中找出下列縮寫詞的每個英文字母代表甚麼字詞。請見示範。

1. SADD <u>Students Against Drunk Driving</u>

2. ASAP _____

3. www _____

4. DVD _____

5. RDA _____

6. mpg _____

3   Interpretation 解釋

3.1 Punctuation Makes A Difference 標點符號的重要

標點符號可以改變一句話的意思。請為以下文章加上正確的標點符號。請在應該大寫的字底下畫線。

earthlings are travellers people all over planet Earth want to visit other places tourists should first see their own country before visiting other ones it looks like people will soon be able to visit other planets as well the words tourist and astronaut may soon mean the same thing

Part 2

Earthquakes
地震

1 Introduction
地動山搖

Timeline 時間軸

1811, 1812
Earthquakes cause the Mississippi River to flow upstream.

1811 ,1812 年
地震讓密西西比河的河水逆流。

1935
Charles Richter invents the Richter Scale to measure the power of earthquakes.

1935 年
查爾斯・黎克特發明了黎克特制震級來測量地震強度。

Where is the Pacific Ring of Fire?
環太平洋火山帶在哪裏？

Pacific Ring of Fire 環太平洋火山帶

DID YOU KNOW? 你知道嗎？

Earthquakes can destroy entire cities. They also cause tsunami and fires, which destroy as much, and sometimes more, as the earthquake itself.

地震能摧毀整個城市。它還會引發破壞力甚至比地震本身更大的海嘯和大火。

KEY TERMS 重點詞彙

tsunami - huge waves created by an earthquake or volcano underwater

海嘯是因地震或海底火山爆發所造成的大浪

shock waves - energy that travels underground, but causes earthquakes at the surface

衝擊波是在地底遊走的能量，能造成地面地震

Pacific Ring of Fire - a band around the Pacific Ocean where two plates meet

環太平洋火山帶是太平洋兩個板塊連接的環狀地帶

Richter Scale - a scale used to measure the strength of earthquakes

黎克特制震級是用來測量地震強度的等級

Chapter One:
Introduction

You hear a rumbling louder than thunder. The ground begins to shake. It's an earthquake!

Earthquakes can be deadly. Many last a minute or less. But in those few seconds entire cities can crumble[1]. Buildings and bridges collapse[2]. People are crushed or buried alive.

Millions have died in earthquakes. Even after an earthquake stops, the damage may continue. Fires break out. These fires can destroy even more than the earthquake itself.

1   crumble, *v*：摧毀
2   collapse, *v*：倒塌

Some earthquakes happen underwater. These can cause big ocean waves called tsunami[1].

Tsunami are huge walls of water. They crash down on land with tremendous[2] force. Tsunami caused by earthquakes kill many thousands of people all over the world.

Tsunami are giant waves that hit the shore. Some are as tall as a ten-storey building. Tsunami are not very big when they are out at sea. But, out in the ocean, they travel faster than a speeding bullet.

Near land, they suck up[3] all the water near the shore. Then they crash down. They can smash and wash away buildings. People are crushed and swept out to sea.

---

1   tsunami, *n*：海嘯
2   tremendous, *adj*：巨大的
3   suck up：吸收

Why Do Earthquakes Happen?

The top layer of our planet is called the crust[1]. It seems solid to us. In fact it's broken into giant pieces. These pieces are called tectonic plates[2].

Plates[3] are always moving. They move very slowly. Sometimes plates slide past each other. Sometimes they push against each other. In some places, plates pull away from each other.

All this movement creates pressure underground. The pressure builds up. It causes huge chunks of rock to break. It's as if a bomb has exploded underground.

An enormous amount of energy is released. Some of this energy is in the form of shock waves[4]. Shock waves travel through the ground. Some of them reach the surface. When they do, they can cause tremendous damage.

---

1   crust, *n*：地殼
2   tectonic plates, *n*：板塊構造
3   plates, *n*：板塊
4   shock waves, *n*：衝擊波

Severe earthquakes can lift huge stones off the ground. The ground can shake so much that buildings tumble down like a house of cards.

Highways crack open. Cars may be swallowed up[1]. It's impossible to stand or run during a bad earthquake. People become helpless. Earthquakes are one of our deadliest natural disasters.

The Pacific Ring of Fire

Most earthquakes happen near where two plates meet. Most of the world's earthquakes occur in a band[2] around the Pacific Ocean. This band is called the Pacific Ring of Fire[3].

Parts of California are on the Pacific Ring of Fire. So is Japan. There are many cities along the Pacific Ring of Fire. When an earthquake hits a big city, it can be a disaster.

---

1   be swallowed up：吞沒
2   band, *n*：地帶
3   Pacific Ring of Fire：環太平洋火山帶

Measuring Earthquakes

There are millions of earthquakes each year. Most of these are very mild[1]. Only about 100,000 can be felt.

Fortunately, only a small fraction[2] of earthquakes cause disasters. Only about 100 cause any damage at all.

There are different ways to measure earthquakes. Scientists use a machine called a seismograph[3] to detect earthquakes. It also measures and records the strength of earthquakes.

The Richter Scale[4] is based on these measurements. Charles Richter[5] developed the Richter Scale in the 1930s. It is the most commonly used scale to rank and measure earthquakes.

1　mild：輕微

2　a small fraction：一小部分

3　seismograph, *n*：地震儀

4　Richter Scale：黎克特制地震震級

5　Charles Richter：查爾斯・黎克特

The Richter Scale goes from 0 to 9. Serious earthquakes usually measure more than 7.0 on the Richter Scale. Earthquakes less than 5.0 rarely cause any damage.

Each number on the scale represents ten times the power of the previous one. So, an earthquake that measures 8.0 on the Richter Scale is ten times more powerful than one that measures 7.0.

Another way to measure earthquakes is to ask people what they felt and saw during an earthquake. The Mercalli Scale[1] is based on what people see and say. It describes how much damage an earthquake causes.

---

1 Mercalli Scale：麥加利地震烈度

The Mercalli Scale:

1. Most people don't feel the earthquake.

2. A few people notice shaking.

3. People indoors think a truck has passed by outside. Hanging objects may swing. People may not realize that it is an earthquake.

4. Windows, dishes, and glasses rattle[1]. People inside may feel a jolt[2] as if something has hit the house. Parked cars rock.

5. Doors swing open and shut. Buildings shake. Liquid slops out[3] of glasses.

---

1   rattle, *v*：發出咯咯聲
2   jolt, *n*：搖動
3   slop out：倒瀉

6. Everyone feels it. Plaster[1] cracks. Things fall off shelves. Windows break. Trees sway.

7. People can't stand up. Loose bricks and tiles tumble down[2].

8. Chimneys[3] fall down. Cracks open in the ground.

9. People panic[4]. Some buildings collapse.

10. Many buildings collapse.

11. The ground cracks open. Train tracks bend and break.

12. All buildings are destroyed. The landscape[5] is totally changed.

---

1 plaster, *n*：水泥
2 tumble down：倒塌
3 chimney, *n*：煙囪
4 panic, *v*：恐慌
5 landscape, *n*：景觀

Earthquake Oddities[1]

An earthquake once made the Mississippi River[2] flow backwards! In 1811 and 1812, there were tremendous earthquakes in the southern states. Water in the great Mississippi River flowed upstream[3] for a short amount of time.

The water flooded forests. It created new lakes. You can still see some of these lakes today. Earthquakes created Reelfoot Lake[4] in Tennessee.[5]

Earthquakes even happen on the moon.

---

1   oddity, *n*：不尋常的事
2   Mississippi River：密西西比河
3   upstream, *adv*：逆流地
4   Reelfoot Lake：里爾富特湖
5   Tennessee：田納西州

But there are not as many as on Earth. And moonquakes are less severe[1]. They occur about halfway between the surface and the centre of the moon.

Snapshot

The moon 月球

---

1 severe, *adj*：嚴重的

2 San Francisco 1906, 1989

火燒舊金山

Timeline 時間軸

April 18, 1906

The Great Earthquake strikes San Francisco a little after 5 a.m.

1906 年 4 月 18 日

舊金山大地震於清晨 5 點左右侵襲舊金山。

October 17, 1989

An earthquake strikes San Francisco. It lasts for 15 seconds.

1989 年 10 月 17 日

地震再次侵襲舊金山，並持續了15秒鐘。

Where is San Francisco? 舊金山在哪裏？ ▶▶▶

SAN FRANCISCO 舊金山

DID YOU KNOW? 你知道嗎？

Between 1975 and 1995, only four states did not have any earthquakes: Florida, Iowa, North Dakota, and Wisconsin.

1975 至 1995 年間，美國只有四個州從未發生過地震：佛羅里達州、愛荷華州、北達科他州、威斯康星州。

KEY TERMS 重點詞彙

fault - a place where two plates scrape against each other

斷層是兩個板塊互相磨擦的地方

rubble - broken pieces of a building

瓦礫堆是建築物的碎片

aftershocks - smaller earthquakes after the main one

餘震是主震之後接連發生的小地震

Chapter Two:
San Francisco, 1906, 1989

San Francisco[1] is a city with a lot of history. In the 1700s, Spanish people came from Mexico. They built a fort[2] there in 1776. It is called the Presidio[3].

The Spanish also built a mission[4]. They named the mission after Saint Francis[5]. They called it San Francisco de Asis[6]. That's how San Francisco got its name.

The Gold Rush

California joined the United States in 1846. There were fewer than a thousand people living there then. Then

---

1　San Francisco：舊金山

2　fort：堡壘

3　Presidio：普瑞斯帝歐要塞

4　mission, *n*：教會

5　Saint Francis：聖・法蘭西斯

6　San Francisco de Asis：阿西西的聖法蘭西斯科教會

some people found gold in California. Thousands rushed to California. They hoped to find gold, too. This was the start of the Gold Rush[1].

San Francisco quickly grew to 20,000 people. The Gold Rush ended. But people still came. San Francisco bay filled with ships.

By 1906, almost half a million people lived there. It was the largest city west of the Missouri River.

There were always earthquakes in San Francisco. People who lived there felt small ones every year. And there were strong ones in 1839, 1865, 1868, 1892, and 1898.

Everyone knew about the earthquakes. But they didn't understand why the ground under their city shook so much.

---

1   Gold Rush：淘金熱

San Andreas Fault

San Francisco is built over a place where two plates meet. The Pacific and North American plates rub and scrape[1] against each other. The strain[2] of this has created the San Andreas Fault[3].

The San Andreas Fault is more than 800 miles long. In some places, you can even see it from the air. It looks like a big, long crack in the ground.

There are also many smaller faults[4] in the area. Some connect to the main fault. Others spread out. This area is one of the weakest parts of the Earth's crust.

There are many earthquakes around the San Andreas Fault. Scientists record about 20,000 tremors[5] every year. Not all cause damage. Most are mild. They don't last very long.

---

1   rub and scrape：互相磨擦
2   strain, *n*：張力
3   San Andreas Fault：聖安德列斯斷層
4   faults, *n*：斷層
5   tremor, *n*：震動

But some are very powerful. Some are strong enough to shake buildings until they break up.

These are the earthquakes people fear. And this is the sort of earthquake that struck[1] San Francisco in 1906.

The Great Earthquake

The Great Earthquake of 1906 began just past 5 a.m. Most were still in bed. A loud rumble[2] woke people up.

Buildings swung from side to side. Furniture tipped over[3] and broke. People were thrown out of bed. Bricks fell from buildings. Windows shattered[4]. People were terrified[5]. They felt helpless. There was nothing they could do.

Chimneys crumbled. There were terrifying crashes as buildings collapsed

---

1   strike, *v*：襲擊
2   rumble, *n*：隆隆聲
3   tipped over：翻倒
4   shatter, *v*：破碎
5   terrified, *adj*：驚嚇

floor by floor. People were crushed under the rubble[1].

The first tremor was the worst. It went on for about one minute. When buildings shook apart, the people inside were crushed. Many died instantly. Others were trapped[2] under the rubble.

Water gushed[3] from burst pipes. It flooded many buildings. The trapped survivors could not escape. Many people drowned[4].

There were also strong aftershocks[5]. Aftershocks happen after an earthquake. The ground shakes again as it settles back down[6].

Already damaged buildings gave way to[7] the aftershocks. Metal trolley tracks[8]

---

1   rubble, n: 瓦礫堆
2   trap, *v*：受困
3   gush, *v*：湧出
4   drown, *v*：淹死
5   aftershock, *n*：餘震
6   settle back down：恢復平靜
7   give way to：屈服於
8   trolley track：有軌電車

twisted up like pretzels[1]. The waterfront was a wreck[2]. Survivors were in shock. But worse was still to come.

Fire!

The earthquake knocked over ovens. It broke gas pipes. There were many gas leaks[3]. Fires broke out all over the city. Gas leaks fueled the flames[4].

There was no water to fight the fires. The earthquake had broken all the water pipes.

People trapped in the ruined buildings burned to death. Eighty people died that way in one hotel.

Fires burned for days. These fires destroyed more than the earthquake itself. Buildings that had survived the earthquake were gutted[5] by fire.

1　pretzel, *n*：蝴蝶餅

2　wreck, n：毀壞

3　leak, *v*：漏氣

4　fueled the flame：火上加油

5　gut, *v*：損毀

The army was called in. They used dynamite[1] to blow up whole streets. They were trying to stop the fire from spreading. Soldiers also shot anyone caught stealing. Many people were killed for looting[2].

Finally, the last fire burned itself out. Most of the city was destroyed.

More than half the city's people were homeless. Most camped out at Golden Gate Park[3]. Others went to the old Spanish Presidio.

Some people thought everyone should leave the city. Why rebuild[4] when another earthquake could happen at any time?

But San Francisco was rebuilt. It now has twice as many people as it did a hundred years ago. And it still has earthquakes.

---

1   dynamite, *n*：炸藥
2   loot, *v*：搶劫
3   Golden Gate Park：金門公園
4   rebuild, *v*：重建

October 17, 1989

The 1906 earthquake measured 8.3 on the Richter Scale. That's an enormous earthquake. But even a smaller earthquake can cause a tremendous amount of damage. This is especially true when it hits a busy city like modern-day San Francisco.

The earthquake that struck San Francisco on October 17, 1989 measured 7.1 on the Richter Scale. That's less than one-tenth as powerful as the 1906 earthquake.

The 1989 earthquake lasted only fifteen seconds. But it caused an elevated highway to collapse. Huge chunks[1] of concrete[2] fell onto cars below. Forty two people died.

The 1989 earthquake caused at least $6 billion dollars worth of damage. Many of the city's old wooden buildings collapsed. 12,000 people became homeless. The San Andreas Fault had struck again.

1　chunk, *n*：大塊
2　concrete, *n*：水泥

The Next Big One?

The San Andreas Fault runs almost the entire length of California. Millions of people live in places at high risk[1] for earthquakes. We can't stop earthquakes. But we can work to lessen their damage.

Modern office buildings in California are built to withstand[2] tremors. They can stay standing even during a big earthquake. Children practice earthquake drills[3] in school. They learn what to do when there is an earthquake.

Scientists watch the San Andreas Fault. They try to predict when and where the next big earthquake will hit. They use laser beams[4] to watch the plates for movement.

1　risk, *n*：風險
2　withstand, *v*：經得起
3　drill, *n*：演習
4　laser beam, *n*：鐳射光

Sometimes there are changes in underground water before an earthquake. These changes result from shifting[1] rocks. So scientists check water levels[2] in wells. They also look for unusual minerals[3] and gases in the water.

But even so, predicting earthquakes is very difficult. It's still a mystery when and where the next big one will hit.

---

1   shift, *adj*：移動的
2   water level：水位
3   mineral, *n*：礦物

California Earthquake Facts

The earliest reported earthquake in California was in 1769. It was felt by a group of explorers[1]. They were camping about 30 miles from Los Angeles[2].

The San Andreas Fault is always moving. But it moves very slowly. It moves about two inches a year. This is about the same rate at which your fingernails grow.

---

1   explorer, *n*：探險家
2   Los Angeles：洛杉磯

Snapshot

The Transamerica Pyramid office building in San Francisco was designed to survive a major earthquake.

舊金山的泛美金字塔辦公大廈採用抗震建築抵抗地震。

99

3 Mexico City, 1985
墨西哥城瓦礫堆中的奇蹟

Timeline 時間軸

1521
Spanish soldiers destroy the Mexican city Tenochtitlán.

1521 年
西班牙士兵摧毀了墨西哥城市特諾奇蒂特蘭。

September 19, 1985
An earthquake shakes Mexico City. The shock waves are stronger than an atomic bomb.

1985 年 9 月 19 日
地震侵襲墨西哥城，衝擊波比原子彈的威力還強。

Where is Mexico City? 墨西哥城在哪裏？▶▶▶

MEXICO CITY 墨西哥城

DID YOU KNOW? 你知道嗎？

When the earthquake hit Mexico City, a hospital collapsed. Babies were rescued after a week of being buried in the rubble!

墨西哥城發生地震後，一所醫院倒塌。有些嬰兒被埋於瓦礫堆中一週後才獲救。

KEY TERMS 重點詞彙

Tenochtitlán - possibly the largest city in the fourteenth-century world; built on islands in Lake Texcoco, Mexico

特諾奇蒂特蘭可能是十四世紀時最大的城市，在墨西哥特斯科科湖的島上建成。

lake bed - the ground at the bottom of a lake

湖床是湖底的地面

Chapter Three:
Mexico City, 1985

Mexico is in North America. It was once part of the Aztec Empire[1]. The Aztecs were Native Americans[2]. Around 1325, the Aztecs built a city on an island in Lake Texcoco[3].

They called it Tenochtitlán[4]. Tenochtitlán became a city of islands. The Aztecs used boats to travel from one part of the city to another.

Tenochtitlán was the capital of the Aztec Empire. The Aztecs ruled much of Mexico for about two hundred years.

---

1   Aztec Empire：阿茲特克帝國
2   Native Americans：美國原住民
3   Lake Texcoco：特斯科科湖
4   Tenochtitlán：特諾奇蒂特蘭

Tenochtitlán was perhaps the largest city in the world. It had a huge temple complex[1]. There was also a royal palace.

Spanish soldiers invaded[2] in 1521. They conquered[3] the Aztecs. They destroyed Tenochtitlán. The Spanish built Mexico City on the ruins[4] of the old Aztec city.

Lake Texcoco dried up. Mexico City spread out over the dry lake bed[5]. More and more people came to live there. By 1985, it was a huge city. About 18 million people lived and worked there.

The lake bed under Mexico City is mostly mud and clay[6]. It is very soft. Soft ground shakes more than hard rock during an earthquake. This means more earthquake damage to buildings built on soft ground.

1　temple complex：寺廟羣

2　invade, *v*：侵略

3　conquer, *v*：征服

4　ruin, *n*：廢墟

5　lake bed：湖床

6　clay, *n*：黏土

The Earthquake

On September 19, 1985, there was a massive[1] earthquake. There were two jolts.

Rocks slipped[2] along a 124-mile fault. This happened about 12 miles below the surface.

The earthquake released tremendous shock waves. These shock waves were more powerful than an atomic bomb[3]. The earthquake measured 8.1 on the Richter Scale.

More than 400 buildings in Mexico City collapsed within five minutes of the first tremor. 3,000 more were badly damaged. Some of these were large high-rise apartments[4].

More than 30,000 people were badly hurt. At least 100,000 people lost their homes. Reports said that 10,000 people

---

1   massive, *adj*：強烈的
2   slip, *v*：滑動
3   atomic bomb：原子彈
4   high-rise apartment：高樓大廈

died. But the exact number may never be known.

The Search for Survivors

After the earthquake, rescue workers[1] searched the wreckage[2]. Survivors were trapped for days in collapsed buildings.

Some rescue equipment[3] can sense body heat. That tells the rescuers where to look. But this equipment is costly. It can be hard to get.

The Mexicans did not have a lot of basic rescue equipment. There weren't enough cranes[4]. There weren't enough saws[5] to cut through concrete. They couldn't move the rubble safely.

Rescue workers sometimes die trying to save others. It is very dangerous work. Still they managed to pull many people

---

1   rescue workers：救援者
2   wreckage, *n*：殘骸
3   equipment, *n*：裝備
4   crane, *n*：起重機
5   saw, *n*：鋸子

out alive. They rescued families from the apartment buildings. But many more died because they could not be rescued in time.

Amazing Survival Stories

One of the buildings that collapsed was a hospital. The top floors fell onto the ones below. Many patients[1] were crushed to death.

There were many newborn babies in the hospital nursery[2]. Many of these babies survived after being buried for seven days. More than 50 infants[3] were rescued alive.

The highest office building in Mexico survived. All 52 floors are still standing. It survived the shock waves of the 1985 earthquake.

---

1 patient, *n*：病人
2 nursery, *n*：育嬰室
3 infant, *n*：嬰兒

Snapshot

Rescue workers pull a body out from the rubble of a building destroyed by an earthquake in Mexico City.

救援者從墨西哥地震摧毀的建築瓦礫堆中救出傷者。

4 Japan, 1923, 1995

日本強震大火奪家園

Timeline 時間軸

September 1, 1923

More than 100,000 people die when an earthquake hits Tokyo, Japan.

1923 年 9 月 1 日
十幾萬人在日本東京大地震中喪生。

January 17, 1995

An earthquake measuring 7.2 on the Richter Scale strikes Kobe, Japan.

1995 年 1 月 17 日
黎克特制震級 7.2 級的地震侵襲日本神戶。

Where is Tokyo? 東京在哪裏？

TOKYO 東京

DID YOU KNOW? 你知道嗎？

During the 1923 earthquake, a woman saved herself and her baby by standing in the water all day. She held her baby on top of her head.

1923年地震時，一個女人將她孩子放在頭頂，在水中站一整天才獲救。

KEY TERMS 重點詞彙

scorch - to burn

使燒焦

epicentre - the ground above where the earthquake starts

震央是地震發生時震源上地面的位置

Chapter Four:
Japan, 1923, 1995

Japan is a country of islands. These islands are on the Pacific Ring of Fire. There are many active volcanoes[1] in Japan.

Japan also has lots of earthquakes. Most are mild. But some are very deadly.

Tokyo, September 1, 1923

Tokyo is the capital city of Japan. It is located on Honshu, Japan's largest island.

In 1923, Tokyo was the fifth largest city in the world. More than 2.5 million people lived there.

That year, a violent[2] earthquake shook most of Honshu[3]. The earthquake measured 8.3 on the Richter Scale.

---

1   active volcano：活火山
2   violent, *adj*：猛烈的
3   Honshu：本州

The shaking was very intense[1]. It registered as high as 12 on the Mercalli Scale. That's the highest possible rating.

Thousands of homes in Tokyo crumpled[2] instantly. Roofs caved in[3] on people. Cooking stoves were smashed. Fires broke out[4].

The Tokyo fires were much worse than the ones in San Francisco after the 1906 earthquake. The fires grew and spread quickly. Thousands who survived the earthquake were burned to death.

People tried to escape the blaze[5]. Many ran to parks. They hoped the fire wouldn't follow them there.

Some people stood up to their necks in water. One woman saved herself and her baby this way. She stood in the water all day holding her baby on top of her head.

---

1   intense, *adj*：劇烈的
2   crumple, *v*：倒坍
3   cave in：塌落
4   break out：爆發
5   blaze, *n*：火焰

Others were not so lucky. Flames blew over the water. The fire scorched[1] their heads and they died. But under the water, their bodies were untouched.

Tokyo was not the only city affected by the earthquake. The port city[2] of Yokohama[3] was also destroyed.

Fires broke out in Yokohama, too. People ran to the sea. But many oil tanks[4] had burst. Burning oil covered the surface of the water.

The earthquake also caused a tsunami. Altogether, about 143,000 people died. 100,000 were in Tokyo. Fires killed about half the people.

Half a million homes were destroyed. The earthquake and fire made more than a million people homeless overnight[5].

---

1   scorch, *v*：使燒焦

2   port city：港市

3   Yokohama: 橫濱市

4   oil tank：油罐

5   overnight, *adv*：一夜之間

Some parents lost their children. Children became orphans[1]. People searched for days for lost relatives.

The fiery-hot[2] air burned people's throats[3]. They could not speak. Instead they held out pieces of paper with their names written out.

Finally, the fires ended. People searched the ashes of their homes for lost possessions[4]. But the fire left very little for them to find.

---

1   orphan, *n*：孤兒

2   fiery-hot, *adj*：火熱的

3   throat, *n*：喉嚨

4   possessions, *n*：財產

Japan Earthquake Facts

September 1st is Disaster Prevention Day in Tokyo. Special memorial services[1] are held in honour of[2] the victims of the 1923 earthquake.

The 1923 earthquake also caused massive landslides[3] in the nearby mountains.

The 1923 earthquake was actually underneath the water. The epicentre[4] was in Sagami Bay[5], which is about 50 miles from Tokyo.

1　memorial service：追悼會
2　in honour of：向…致敬
3　landslide, *n*：山崩
4　epicentre, *n*：震央
5　Sagami Bay：相模灣

Kobe, 1995

A sudden and severe earthquake shook Honshu again on January 17, 1995. This time the earthquake was centred near the south of the island. The industrial port city of Kobe[1] was hardest hit.

The 1995 earthquake measured 7.2 on the Richter Scale. It shook the city of Kobe for 20 seconds.

Broken gas pipes burst into flames[2] all over the city. Water pipes burst.

About 5,500 people were killed. 100,000 buildings were destroyed.

Many of the newer buildings survived. They had been built with earthquakes in mind[3].

---

1 Kobe：神戶
2 burst into flames：燃起大火
3 in mind：顧慮到

5 Lisbon, 1755
巨浪席捲里斯本

Timeline 時間軸

1754

The French and Indian War begins.

1754 年
法國－印地安人戰爭開始。

November 1, 1755

Lisbon, Portugal, is destroyed by an earthquake, followed by fires and tsunami.

1755 年 11 月 1 日
地震和地震引發的海嘯及大火摧毀葡萄牙里斯本。

Where is Lisbon? 里斯本在哪裏？ ▶▶▶

LISBON 里斯本

DID YOU KNOW? 你知道嗎？

Tidal waves and tsunami are both huge waves. But a tidal wave is caused by high winds. A tsunami is caused by an underwater earthquake or volcanic eruption.

潮波和海嘯都是大浪。但大風引發潮波。海底地震和火山爆發則引發海嘯。

KEY TERMS 重點詞彙

harbour - a place where boats dock to be safe from storms

港灣是指船隻靠岸，安全避風雨的地方

priceless - too valuable to have a price

無價，即是很貴重的

capsize - to overturn

傾覆是弄翻的意思

Chapter Five:
Lisbon, 1755

Lisbon[1] became the capital city of Portugal[2] in 1256. It was the main port city for the Portuguese Empire. By 1755, it was home to more than a quarter of a million people.

Lisbon was one of the largest and most beautiful cities in Europe. It had a busy harbour on the Tagus River[3]. There were castles, churches, and a grand cathedral[4].

The Earthquake

On November 1, 1755, a powerful earthquake hit Lisbon. It was a holiday. Many people were in the city's churches.

---

1   Lisbon：里斯本
2   Portugal：葡萄牙
3   Tagus River：塔霍河
4   cathedral, *n*：大教堂

They were lighting candles for All Saints Day[1].

At 9:40 a.m., there was a loud rumble[2]. People were frightened. They ran outside. But what they saw was even more terrifying.

The earthquake was pushing the ground up into the air. People couldn't stand or walk. Everyone panicked. But there was nothing they could do.

Buildings collapsed all over the city. Thousands were killed instantly. Many survivors rushed toward the river. Some jumped onto ships. They hoped to escape.

Others gathered on the new stone pier[3] that ran along the river's edge. They thought they would be safe there. But they were wrong.

---

1 All Saints Day：諸聖節
2 rumble, *n*：隆隆聲
3 pier, *n*：防波堤

Tsunami

Three tsunami travelled from the Atlantic Ocean[1] to the Tagus River. They crashed into Lisbon Harbour. The people on the pier were washed away. Boats capsized[2]. Many drowned.

Fire

Still, the disaster continued. Hundreds of fires burned in the city. Some were started by overturned[3] candles. Others were caused by cooking stoves and lamps.

Fires burned for days. When the smoke finally cleared, the city was a complete ruin. More than 60,000 people had died.

---

1 Atlantic Ocean：大西洋

2 capsize, *v*：傾覆翻船

3 overturn, *v*：翻倒

City in Ruins

The fire and earthquake destroyed most of Lisbon. The tsunami wrecked the waterfront[1]. More than half the city's churches were totally ruined. The rest were badly damaged. Many priceless[2] works of art were also destroyed.

Many survivors left the city. Their experience was too awful[3] for them to stay.

The Richter Scale had not yet been invented. Scientists estimate that the Lisbon earthquake was about 8.7 on the Richter Scale.

---

1   waterfront, *n*：濱水區
2   priceless, *adj*：珍貴的
3   awful, *adj*：可怕的

6 China
中國唐山大地震

Timeline 時間軸

1831 BCE
Earliest recorded earthquake occurs.

公元前 1831 年
最早的地震記錄。

July 28, 1976
The deadliest earthquake of the twentieth century hits Tangshan, China.

1976 年 7 月 28 日
20 世紀最具毀滅性的地震侵襲中國唐山。

Where is Tangshan? 唐山在哪裏？

TANGSHAN 唐山

DID YOU KNOW? 你知道嗎？

The aftershock of the 1976 Tangshan earthquake did more damage than the first one.

1976年唐山大地震餘震比主震造成的破壞更大。

KEY TERMS 重點詞彙

BCE - Before Common Era

公元前

eyewitness - a person who sees something happen

目擊者是親眼目睹事件發生的人

rupture - to burst or break

破裂

Chapter Six:
China

China has a long history of earthquakes. Some of the deadliest earthquakes ever have happened in China.

We don't know a lot about ancient earthquakes. Back then[1], only a few people then had a written language. This means there are very few records of ancient earthquakes.

The Chinese had a written language long before most others. They wrote down many things. They also recorded earthquakes. Many of these records were lost. But some survived.

The earliest recorded earthquake happened in China. It was in 1831 BCE[2]. That's almost four thousand years ago!

1　back then：那時
2　BCE：公元前

Key Dates

1831 BCE: The earliest recorded earthquake in the world happens in China.

780 BCE: The Chinese began a complete record of Chinese earthquakes.

1556: More than 800,000 people die in an earthquake.

1920: An earthquake starts a landslide. 200,000 people die.

1927: An earthquake that measures 8.3 on the Richter Scale kills about 200,000 people.

1976: An earthquake hits near Tangshan[1]. Reports from China say that 255,000 people died. But some say more than twice that number died.

---

1 Tangshan：唐山

There are no other records of Chinese earthquakes that happened long ago. But there are more complete records of earthquakes starting in 780 BCE.

The world's deadliest recorded earthquake happened in 1556. It struck in central China.

Most people there lived in caves[1]. They carved their homes out of soft rock. The caves collapsed during the earthquake. About 830,000 people were killed.

Preventing Disaster

We can't stop earthquakes. But we can sometimes predict[2] them. Scientists know several warning signs[3] that an earthquake is about to[4] happen.

One of these is a change in underground water levels. Sometimes rocks move around just before an earthquake. This

---

1 cave, *n*：洞穴
2 predict, *v*：預測
3 warning sign, *n*：前兆
4 about to：即將

causes water underground to move, too.

In early February, 1975, a radio broad-cast[1] warned the residents of Haicheng[2] to leave immediately. Scientists had noticed that water levels in wells were changing. Then there were small tremors.

On February 4 there was a powerful earthquake. It measured 7.5 on the Richter Scale. Thousands of buildings collapsed. Some people died. But it could have been much deadlier without the warning.

A successful earthquake prediction is a great achievement[3]. It can save thousands of lives. But scientists can't predict every earthquake.

China suffered another powerful earthquake a year later. This time there was no warning. It came as a surprise, a very deadly surprise.

---

1   radio broadcast, *n*：電台廣播
2   Haicheng：海城
3   achievement, *n*：成就

1976, Tangshan

On July 28, 1976, an earthquake struck the city of Tangshan. The earthquake happened in the middle of the night. Almost everyone was asleep.

Eyewitnesses[1] saw a bright flash across the sky. That was followed by a deafening roar[2]. Then the shaking began.

Roofs caved in. Some concrete buildings collapsed. The top floors fell onto the ones below. People were crushed to death without even waking up.

It was almost impossible to rescue people in the dark. The earthquake had knocked out the power[3]. There were no lights. It was pitch-black outside. Many people died before they could be saved.

1　eyewitness, *n*：目擊者

2　deafening roar：震耳欲聾

3　knocked out the power：癱瘓電力

The earthquake measured 8.2 on the Richter Scale. It happened along a 150-km (93-mile) fault. The entire fault ruptured[1]. That released a huge amount of energy. Powerful shock waves rippled out[2] underground.

This massive earthquake may have triggered[3] a second one. There was an aftershock about 16 hours later. It struck the same area. This second earthquake measured at least 7.6 on the Richter Scale.

Many of Tangshan's newer buildings survived the first earthquake. But the second earthquake did even more damage than the first. Everything was flattened[4]. The city was totally destroyed. No buildings were left standing.

---

1 rupture, *v*：破裂
2 ripple out：泛起漣漪
3 trigger, *v*：觸發
4 flatten, *v*：鏟平

Some workers were trapped in nearby coal mines[1]. They were stuck under ground for hours or days. But many of them were finally rescued.

The Chinese government said that more than 600,000 people were badly hurt, and about a quarter million died. More recent studies say that closer to half a million died. Either way, this was the deadliest quake in the twentieth century.

---

1   coal mine, *n*：煤礦場

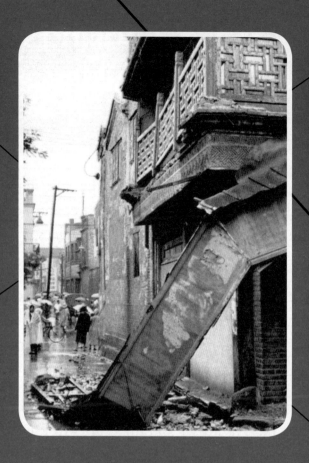

Snapshot

Damaged buildings in a popular shopping district near Beijing after the 1976 earthquake in Tangshan.

1976年唐山大地震後，北京附近的商場建築物倒塌毀壞。

7 Preparing for Earthquakes

防患未然

The U.S. Geological Survey[1] has an Earthquake Hazards Program. They try to prepare people for earthquakes. They also have other services.

For example, they can send you an email every time a big earthquake strikes. They report earthquakes of 4.5 magnitude[2] or greater if they occur in the United States. And they report earthquakes of 5.5 magnitude or greater if they occur anywhere else in the world.

Have you ever felt the ground shake? If so, the Earthquake Hazards Program[3] wants to know! Check out "Did you feel it?" at http://pasadena.wr.usgs.gov/shake. In the future, if you feel an earthquake, you can report it on their website. This information helps the USGS learn more about earthquakes.

1　U.S. Geological Survey：(USGS) 美國地質勘探局

2　magnitude, *n*：震級

3　Earthquake Hazards Program：地震災難計劃

Exercises 練習

1 Vocabulary 詞彙

1.1 Word Sort 詞彙分類

將下面詞彙分類為複合詞及非複合詞。請見示範。

underwater	shock waves	damage	highways
helpless	underground	outside	indoors
moonquakes	halfway	itself	homeless
aftershocks	waterfront	high-rise	homeless
wreckage	landslides	overturned	

Compound words:
underwater _____

_____

_____

_____

Other Words
damage _____

_____

_____

_____

1.2 Fill in the Blanks 填充

使用本書出現的詞彙做以下填充題。

Sometimes, the Earth shakes only a little bit. These little shakes or (1) ____ are too small to be called earthquakes. Earthquakes underwater are called (2) ____

_____. They may seem small in the middle of the ocean, but by the time they get to land, they are (3) _____. Scientists use a machine called a (4) _____ to measure the strength of a quake. Often, an earthquake is followed by smaller quakes called (5) _____ _____. Scientists use the (6) _____ scale to measure how strong a quake is. Another scale used is the (7) _____ scale. The (8) _____ is the place underground where a quake first begins.

2 Initial Understanding 初步理解

2.1 True or False? 是非題

判斷左方的句子是否正確。

1. Quakes can cause other disasters to occur.   T F

2. Earthquakes only happen around the Pacific Ocean.   T F

3. Sometimes warnings signal that a quake is about to happen.   T F

4. Quakes can never happen in the same place twice.   T F

5. Earthquakes always kill people.   T F

6. Everything falls down during a strong quake.   T F

7. The moon also experiences quakes.   T F

8. Movement in the Earth's crust causes tremors.   T   F

9. Scientists only know about recent quakes.   T   F

10. There is more than one way to measure an earthquake.   T   F

3   Interpretation 解釋

3.1 Before, During, After 事發前後與經過

選取本書其中一個地震。寫至少五個單詞描寫地震之前，地震當時，和地震之後的情景（人、事、物、景觀）。

Before	During	After
peaceful	loud	burning

135

Answer Key 答案

Part 1

1.1 Multiple Meaning Words

1. A, 2. B, 3. B, 4. B, 5. A, 6. B, 7. B

2.1 Acronyms

除了 4. Mir 全部打勾

1. E, 2. B, 3. A, 4. D, 5. C

2.2 Everyday Acronyms

1. Students Against Drunk Driving
2. As soon as possible
3. world wide web
4. digital video disc
5. recommended daily allowance
6. miles per gallon

3.1 Punctuation Makes A Difference

Earthlings are travellers. People all over planet Earth want to visit other places. Tourists should first see their own country before visiting other ones. It looks like people will soon be able to visit other planets as well. The words tourist and astronaut may soon mean the same thing!

Part 2

1.1 Word Sort

Compound words: underwater, shock waves, highways, underground, outside, indoors, moonquakes, halfway, itself, aftershocks, waterfront, high-rise, landslides, overturned

Other words with sample reasons: damage – dams and age do not have anything to do with something that is damaged or broken; helpless -*less is a suffix*; homeless-*less is a suffix*; wreckage-*age is a suffix*

Sample rule: If the words put together do not lose the meaning of the original separate words, they probably form a compound word.

1.2 Fill in the Blanks

1. tremors; 2. tsunami;
3. tremendous or enormous;
4. seismograph; 5. aftershocks;
6. Richter; 7. Mercalli; 8. epicentre

2.1 True or False?

1. T; 2. F; 3. T; 4. F; 5. F; 6. F;
7. T; 8. T; 9. F; 10. T

3.1 Before, During, After

Sample answers:

Before: peaceful, dry, calm, still, quiet, unconcerned, strong

During: loud, rumbling, panicked, scared, moving, shifting, flooded

After: burning, fallen, injured, wrecked, careful, hopeful, shaky, quiet

English-Chinese Vocabulary List
中英對照生詞表

Proper names
專有名詞

Administration (NASA), 美國
太空總署 (美國宇航局)

Air Force
空軍

Aldrin, Buzz
奧爾德林 · 巴茲

All Saints Day
諸聖節

Apollo 1
阿波羅 1 號

Apollo 13
阿波羅 13 號

Armstrong, Neil
阿姆斯壯 · 尼爾

Atlantic Ocean
大西洋

Australia
澳洲

Aztec Empire
阿茲特克帝國

BCE
西元前

California 加州

Challenger
挑戰者號

China
中國

Columbia
哥倫比亞號

Earth
地球

Earthquake Hazards Program
地震災難計劃

Educator Astronaut Program 太
空人老師計劃

Endeavour
奮進號

Gagarin, Yuri
加加林 · 尤里

German measles
德國痲疹

Gold Rush
淘金熱

Golden Gate Park
金門公園

Haicheng
海城

Honshu
本州

Idaho
愛達荷州

International Space Station
(ISS) 國際太空站 (國際空
間站)

Israel
以色列

Japan
日本

Kennedy , John F.
甘迺迪 · 約翰

Kobe
神戶

Lake Texcoco
特斯科科湖

Lisbon
里斯本

Los Angeles
洛杉磯

McAuliffe, Sharon Christa
麥考利芙 · 莎倫 ·
克里斯塔

Mexico City
墨西哥城

Mexico
墨西哥

Mir
和平號

Mission Control
任務控制中心

Mississippi River
密西西比河

Morgan, Barbara
摩根 · 芭芭拉

National Aeronautics and Space
Administration
美國太空總署

Native Americans
美國原住民

New Hampshire
新罕布什爾州

Pacific Ring of Fire
環太平洋火山帶

Portugal
葡萄牙

Presidio
普瑞斯帝歐要塞

Reelfoot Lake
里爾富特湖

Richter Scale
黎克特制地震震級/
芮氏地震規模 (里氏震級)

Russian
俄羅斯人

139

Sagami Bay
相模灣

Saint Francis
聖・法蘭西斯

Salyut 1
敬禮 1 號

San Andreas Fault
聖安德列斯斷層

San Francisco de Asis
阿西西的聖法蘭西斯科
教會

San Francisco
舊金山

Skylab
天空實驗室

Soviet Union
蘇聯

Soyuz
聯合號

Tagus River
塔霍河

Tangshan
唐山

Teacher in Space
Program (TISP)
太空教師計劃

Tennessee
田納西州

Tenochtitlán
特諾奇蒂特蘭

Tokyo
東京

USGS
美國地質勘探局

Yokohama
濱市

Mexico City
墨西哥城

Mexico
墨西哥

General Vocabulary
一般詞彙

about to
即將

accident
意外

achievement
成就

active volcano
活火山

aftershock
餘震

astronaut
太空人

atomic bomb
原子彈

awful
可怕的

back-up pilot
後備駕駛員

bail out
逃脱

band
地帶

bang
砰的一聲

blast off
發射

blaze
火焰

blow apart
爆炸解體

board
登機

bone
骨頭

boom
隆隆聲

booster
助推器

break out
爆發；起火

breathe
呼吸

broadcast live
現場直播

capital
首都

capsize
傾覆翻船

catastrophe
大災難

catch up to
趕上

cathedral
大教堂

cave in
塌落

cave
洞穴

central
中部

chimney
煙囱

circumstance
情勢

clay
黏土

coal mine
煤礦場

cockpit
駕駛員座艙

collapse
倒塌

colonel
上校

command module
指揮艙

commander
指揮官

communications system
通訊系統

compete against
競爭

concrete
水泥

conduct
執行

conquer 征服

consist of
包括

cosmonaut
前蘇聯太空人 (宇航員)

crane
起重機

crew
組員

crumble
摧毀；倒塌

crumple
倒塌

crust
地殼

deafening roar
震耳欲聾的轟鳴

dehydrated
脫水的

clay
黏土

coal mine
煤礦場

cockpit
駕駛員座艙

collapse
倒塌

colonel
上校

command module
指揮艙

commander
指揮官

communications system
通訊系統

compete against
競爭

delay
延誤

depend on
依賴

design
設計

disappointed
失望

disaster
災難

drill
演習

drown
淹死

dynamite
炸藥

electrical wiring
電路

electricity
電力

emergency
緊急事故

energy
能量

epicentre
震央

equipment
設備

escape
逃脫

estimate
估計

excellent
傑出的

experienced
有經驗的

experiment
實驗

explanation
解釋

explode
爆炸

explorer
探險家

explosion
爆炸

expose to
使感染

extraordinary
特別的

eyewitness
目擊者

failure
失敗

fantasy
幻想

fast-release escape hatch
速開逃生門

fault
故障

faults
斷層

fiery-hot
火熱的

fire
火災

fire extinguisher
滅火器

flatten
鏟平

fleet
機羣

foam
泡沫材料

forecast
預報

freezing
極冷的

fuel supply
燃料電池

fuel the flame
火上加油

gas mask
防毒面具

get used to
熟悉

give way to
屈服於

gravity
地球引力

ground
擱淺

gush
湧出

gut
損毀

halfway between
位於…中間

harbour
港灣

hatch
艙門

heart attack
心臟病發

hero
英雄

high school
高中

high-rise apartment
高樓大廈

ignite
使燃燒

in flight
飛行中

in honour of
向…致敬

in memory of
為了紀念

in mind
顧慮到

industrial
工業的

infant
嬰兒

intense
強烈的

invade
侵略

investigation
調查

jolt
搖動

knocked out the power
癱瘓電力

laboratory
實驗室

lake bed
湖床

landscape
景觀

landslide
山崩

laser beam
鐳射光

launch
發射

leak
漏氣

lifeboat
逃生艇

lift off
升空

load
貨物

loot
搶劫

lunar module
登月艙

magnitude
震級

massive
強烈的

melt
熔化

memorial service
追悼會

mineral
礦物

mission
教會

nursery
育嬰室

oil tank
油罐

orbit
繞軌道運行

orphan
孤兒

oven
烤箱

overnight
一夜之間

overturn
翻倒

panic
恐慌

patient
病人

pier
防波堤

pilot
駕駛

plaster
水泥

plates
板塊

port city
港市

possessions
財產

predict
預測

pressure
壓力

pretzel
蝴蝶餅

priceless
珍貴的

142

radio broadcast
電台廣播

rattle
發出咯咯聲

rebuild
重建

record
記錄

release
釋放

rescue workers
救援者

ripple out
泛起漣漪

risk 風險

royal palace
皇宮

rub and scrape
互相磨擦

rubble
瓦礫堆

ruin 廢墟

rumble
隆隆聲

rupture
破裂

saw
鋸子

scorch
使燒焦

seismograph
地震儀

settle back down
恢復平靜

severe
嚴重的

shatter
破碎

shift
移動的

shock waves
衝擊波

slip
滑動

slop out
倒瀉

strain
張力

strike
襲擊

suck up
吸收

survivor
生還者

swallowed up, be
吞沒

tectonic plates
板塊構造

temple complex
寺廟羣

terrified
驚嚇

thousands
成千上萬的人

throat
喉嚨

tipped over
翻倒

trap
受困

tremendous
巨大的

tremor
震動

trigger
觸發

trolley track
有軌電車

tsunami
海嘯

tumble down
倒塌

upstream
逆流地

victim
死難者

violent
猛烈的

warning sign
前兆

water level
水位

waterfront
濱水區

withstand
禁得起

More to Read 延伸閱讀

Bredeson, Carmen. *The Challenger Disaster: Tragic Space Flight.* American Disasters. Springfield, NJ: Enslow Publishers, 1999.

Brubaker, Paul. *Apollo 1 Tragedy: Fire in the Capsule.* American Disasters. Berkeley Heights, NJ: Enslow Publishers, 2002.

Dalgleish, Sharon. *Earthquakes.* Junior Adventure. Broomall, PA: Mason Crest Publishers, 2003.

Gallant, Roy A. *Plates: Restless Earth.* Earthworks. New York: Benchmark Books, 2003.

Landau, Elaine. *Space Disasters.* Watts Library. New York: Franklin Watts, 1999.

Luke, Thompson. *Earthquakes.* High Interest Books. New York: Children's Press, 2000.

Pentland, Peter and Pennie Stoyles. *Earth Science.* Philadelphia: Chelsea House Publishers, 2003.

Stidworthy, John. *Earthquakes & Volcanoes.* The Changing World. San Diego: Thunder Bay Press, 1996.

Stott, Carole. *Space Exploration. Eyewitness Books.* New York: Dorling Kindersley, 2000.

Van Rose, Susanna. *Volcano & Earthquake.* Eyewitness Books. New York: Alfred A. Knopf, 2000.

Vogt, Gregory. *Disasters in Space Exploration.* Brookfield, CT: Millbrook Press, 2001.